THE MYSTERY
OF THE
GOLDEN PYRAMID

ADELA NOREAN   AARON CUSHLEY

When Sophie walked into the bedroom of her
new house she got a tremendous shock.

"A dog!" she cried.
"My name is Ari," the dog replied.
"Pleased to meet you."
"You can TALK?" gasped Sophie. "Are you real?"

Ari nodded. "This casket belongs to you.
It contains the first piece of a puzzle
which only you can solve."

The box sparkled in the sunlight.
Sophie knelt down and lifted the jewelled lid.

"I know that name!"
cried Sophie, reaching
for her book.

She flicked excitedly
through the bright
pages until she found . . .

EGYPTIAN
KINGS

"That's awful. Poor King Nebra,"
sighed Sophie.
Ari nodded. "I have to find
the other amulets.
Will you help me?" he asked.
"Oh yes!" Sophie exclaimed.
"But won't we need the
pharaoh's heir?"
"That's you, Sophie," Ari smiled.
"Only you can help the king."

Sophie's eyes opened wide.
"I'm related to **a king?**"
she gasped.

"Then of course I'll help. Quick!"
She grabbed her bag, and together
they raced out of the door.

They **ran** past bustling shops and houses . . .

The little boat bobbed across the water.

"**Eek!**" squeaked Sophie, as Ari saved her from the jaws of an enormous **crocodile**.

At last they reached the sandy desert on the opposite bank.

The third shook . . .

. . . till they came to the port.
"We'll have to sneak aboard a boat!" called Sophie.

Ari growled. "Anyone who harms the heir of
Nebra will have to face me!"

"The Temple of the Four Pharaohs," said Sophie.
"I hope the first missing amulet is still here!"

"Let's ask th[e]
Sophie gulp[ed]

"We h[ave]

The first statu[e]
shuddered to life

The friends raced
across the desert until
they arrived at the
Palace of the Murals.

They crept into its
dusty interior.

"These murals are so silly," tutted Ari.
"I'm not sure if they'll be any help."

Why are
pharaohs boastful?
They sphinx they
know best!

Mirror, mirror,
in my hand,
Who's the fairest
in the land?

I feel a
little flat
today!

"Hello," Sophie called.
"Please can you give me the
hawk's head amulet?"
But the murals were too
busy chatting to hear her.

. . . to reveal the amulet and a golden pyramid shimmering on the wall.

"That must be where the last amulet is," said Ari. "To the pyramid!"

The sphinxes of the golden pyramid glared down as Sophie and Ari approached.
"This is King Nebra's heir," Ari barked. "I'm guiding her to the heart of the pyramid."

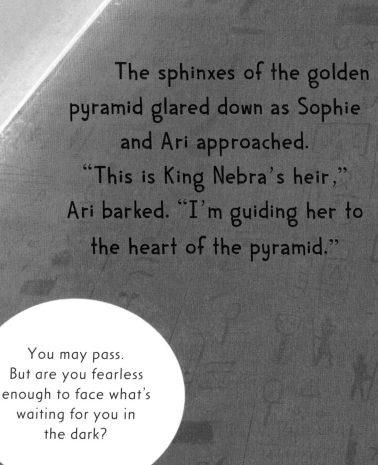

You may pass. But are you fearless enough to face what's waiting for you in the dark?

Sophie gulped.
"I don't like the dark."
"Me neither," replied Ari.
"But together we can do it."

"And we **must** help the king," nodded Sophie.

They scrambled up towards the stone door.

Sophie
flicked on
her torch and
followed Ari

down,

down,

down

the dark

staircase,

along a dusty hall,

They trekked
through rooms and
secret passages . . .

until,

at last,
they
reached
the
chamber of the
goddess Isis.

and up
steep
stone steps.

"Isis protects the king," whispered Ari. "She's fierce."
Suddenly, Sophie's torch flickered and went out. "No!" she gasped.
But there was no turning back, so she stepped into the darkness.

"WHO GOES THERE?"
boomed a deep voice.
"We're returning the pharaoh's
amulets," explained Sophie.
"But we need the last one.
Do you have it?"

"Answer this riddle and it is yours,"
said Isis.

"Sometimes I'm dim,
sometimes I'm bright,
I'm your friend in the darkness,
my name is . . ."

"Stars can bright or dim,"
suggested Ari.

"And they guide sailors . . . like you've guided me,"
added Sophie. "STARS is the answer!"

"WRONG!" roared Isis.
"We can't let the king down," fretted Ari.
"A friend in the darkness . . ." Sophie muttered.
"I know! The answer is LIGHT!"

At once, the room lit up
and a panel of hieroglyphs
appeared.

"The final
amulet must be here,"
said Ari.
"In the middle!"
called Sophie.
"With the king's head!"

At last, she could return
all four precious statues
to the king's tomb.

The pyramid walls
shuddered.
"Ari, I'm scared!"
gasped Sophie as the
door swung open.

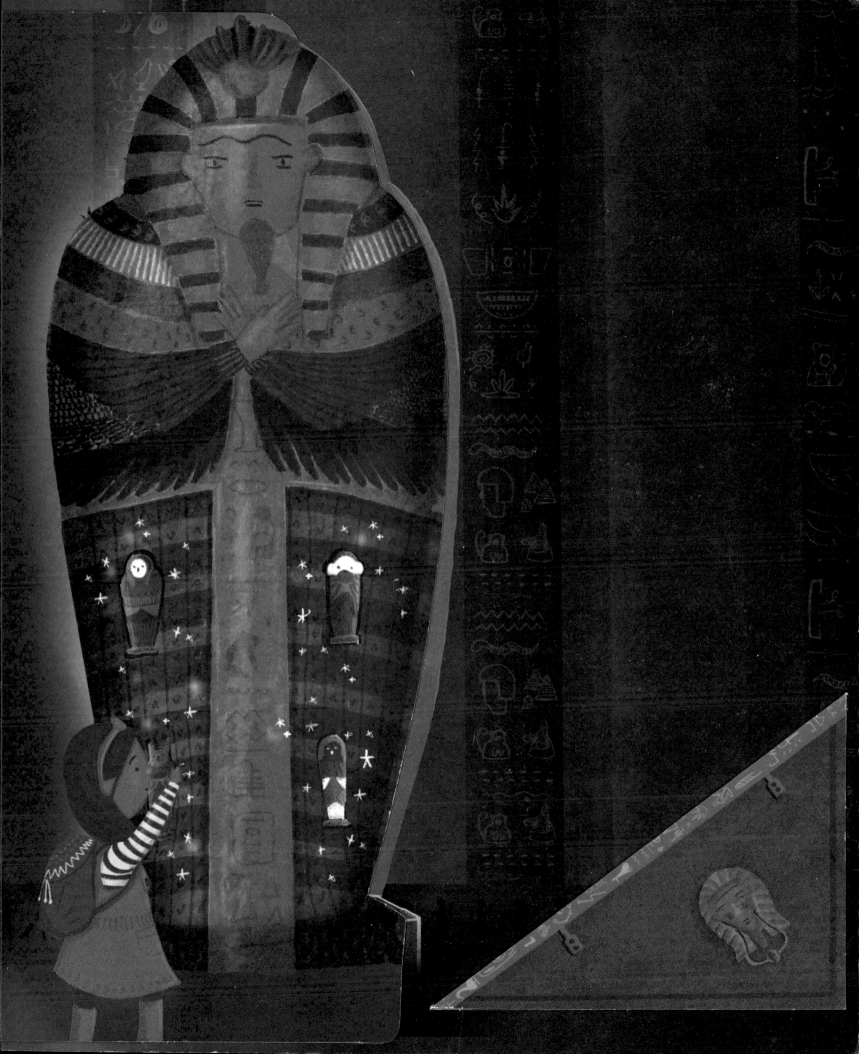

. . . and into the light of Sophie's room.

"Ari! What a day!"
Sophie laughed, giving him a hug.
"I wonder what amazing adventures
will be waiting for us tomorrow?"